Rosie Feels Sick

BY MICHÈLE DUFRESNE

CONTENTS

Pioneer Valley Educational Press, Inc.

Rosie Feels Sick

Rosie was sleeping on her pillow.

"Wake up, Rosie," said Bella. "Come and play."

"No!" said Rosie.
"I don't feel good."

"Oh, no!" said Bella.
"What's wrong?"

"I just feel sick,"
said Rosie.

Bella went and got
her toy elephant.

"Here," said Bella.
"My elephant will make you
feel better."

She put the elephant
next to Rosie.

"Thank you," said Rosie.

Daisy ran into the room
and looked at Rosie.

"Wake up, Rosie,"
said Daisy.
"Come and play with me."

"No!" said Rosie.
"I don't feel good."

Daisy went and got her
toy elephant.

"Here," said Daisy.
"My elephant will make you
feel better."

She put the elephant
next to Rosie.

"Thank you," said Rosie.

Jack ran into the room
and looked at Rosie.

"Wake up, Rosie,"
said Jack.
"Come and play with me."

"No!" said Rosie.
"I don't feel good."

Jack went and got
a sock.

"Here," said Jack.
"This sock will make you
feel better."

He put the sock
next to Rosie.

"Thank you," said Rosie.

Mom took Rosie
to the vet. The vet
looked at Rosie.

"Let's see, Rosie,"
said the vet.
"It looks like a tick
bit you. The tick
made you sick.
Here is some medicine
to make you better."

Rosie took her medicine.

"I feel better," she said.
"Now I can play."

"Did my elephant help
make you feel better?"
asked Bella.

"Yes," said Rosie.

"Did my elephant help
make you feel better?"
asked Daisy.

"Yes," said Rosie.

"Did the sock help
make you feel better?"
asked Jack.

"Oh, yes," said Rosie.
"*Everything* helped
make me feel better!
Come on, let's play!"

Rosie Feels Sick: The Play

Narrator

Rosie was sleeping on her pillow.

Bella

Wake up, Rosie. Come and play.

Rosie

No! I don't feel good.

Bella

Oh, no! What's wrong?

Rosie

I just feel sick.

Bella

Here. My elephant will make you feel better.

Thank you.

Wake up, Rosie.
Come and play
with me.

No! I don't feel good.

Here. My elephant will
make you feel better.

Thank you.

Wake up, Rosie.
Come and play
with me.

Rosie

No! I don't feel good.

Jack

Here. This sock will make you feel better.

Rosie

Thank you.

Narrator

Mom took Rosie to see the vet.

Veterinarian

It looks like a tick bit you. The tick made you sick. Here is some medicine to make you better.

Rosie

I feel better.
Now I can play.

Bella

Did my elephant help make you feel better?

Daisy

Did my elephant help make you feel better?

Jack

Did the sock help make you feel better?

Rosie

Yes! *Everything* helped make me feel better! Come on, let's play!

Ticks

Ticks are tiny bugs.
Baby ticks have 6 legs.
Grown-up ticks have 8 legs,
like spiders.

Ticks do not jump or fly.
They live in tall grass
and bushes.
They attach to animals
that pass by.

Ticks feed on the blood of dogs, cats, birds, and other animals. They can carry diseases. This is how some dogs get sick.

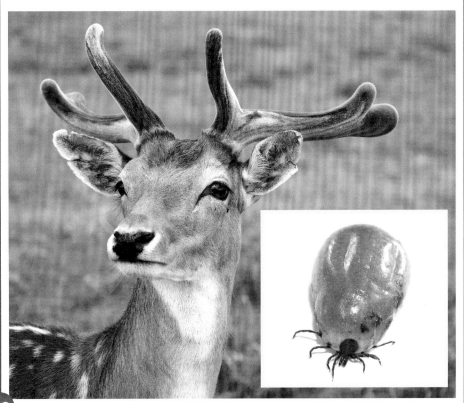